STEP-BY-STEP EXPERIMENTS WITH LIGHT AND VISION

By Ryan Jacobson

Illustrated by Bob Ostrom

The Child's World

Published by The Child's World®
1980 Lookout Drive • Mankato, MN 56003-1705
800-599-READ • www.childsworld.com

ACKNOWLEDGMENTS
The Child's World®: Mary Berendes, Publishing Director
The Design Lab: Design and production
Red Line Editorial: Editorial direction
Consultant: Dr. Peter Barnes, Assistant Scientist, Astronomy Dept.,
    University of Florida

ISBN 9781609735883
LCCN 2011940143

PHOTO CREDITS
Katrina Brown/Dreamstime, cover; Pilar Echeverria/Dreamstime, cover,
back cover; Artem Gorohov/Shutterstock Images, 1, 23; Erik Reis/Shut-
terstock Images, 4; Vlad Turchenko/Shutterstock Images, 8; Shutterstock
Images, 13; Igor Negovelov/Shutterstock Images, 14; Marie C Fields/
Shutterstock Images, 18; Bogdan Ionescu/Shutterstock Images, 24;
David Wigner/Dreamstime, 28

Design elements: Pilar Echeverria/Dreamstime, Robisklp/Dreamstime,
Jeffrey Van Daele/Dreamstime, Sarit Saliman/Dreamstime

Printed in the United States of America

BE SAFE !

The experiments in this book are meant for kids, but sometimes they require an adult's help. Check the supply list of each experiment. It will note if an adult is needed. An adult can also help you find or buy supplies.

TABLE OF CONTENTS

4

Eyes see light that bounces off an object.

CHAPTER ONE

Study Light and Vision!

Look around. Did you know that light is flying through the air? Light is moving energy. It travels very quickly. Light is made up of **wavelengths**. When light shines, it lets out too many wavelengths to count. The wavelengths travel in lines. They go in different directions. They touch each other, too. This makes light shine every which way.

For you to see an object, light needs to hit the object. Then the light will **reflect** off the object. This light travels into your eyes. This is what makes vision possible. Look around again. What do see? Or rather, what reflects light rays into your eyes? How can you learn more about light and vision?

CHAPTER TWO

Seven Science Steps

Doing a science **experiment** is a fun way to discover new facts! An experiment follows steps to find answers to science questions. This book has experiments to help you learn about light and vision. You will follow the same seven steps in each experiment:

6

Seven Steps

1. Research: Figure out the facts before you get started.

2. Question: What do you want to learn?

3. Guess: Make a **prediction**. What do you think will happen in the experiment?

4. Gather: Find the supplies you need for your experiment.

5. Experiment: Follow the directions.

6. Review: Look at the results of the experiment.

7. Conclusion: The experiment is done. Now it is time to reach a **conclusion**. Was your prediction right?

Are you ready to become a scientist? Let's experiment to learn about light and vision!

8

We can see underwater.

CHAPTER THREE

On the Money

Light passes through water. You can see underwater. But things look different than they would on land. The light looks different, too. Try this to see what happens to light in water.

Research the Facts

Here are two. Can you find some more?

- Light moves as a ray of energy. It travels in a straight line.
- Light passes through some objects, such as glass. It bounces off other objects, such as metal.

Ask Questions

- What happens to light rays as they move through water?
- Does water change the way we see things?

9

Make a Prediction

Here are two examples:

- Water makes light rays bend.
- Even in water, light rays move in a straight line.

Gather Your Supplies!

- Coin
- Sticky putty
- Large bowl (not see-through)
- Glass of water
- Pencil or pen
- Paper
- Camera (optional)

Time to Experiment!

1. Grab your coin. Stick a small chunk of sticky putty on one side.

2. Put the bowl on a table. Press the coin into the middle of the bowl. Make sure the sticky putty sticks to the bottom of the bowl. It should hold the coin in place.

3. Step away from the bowl. Stop when you cannot see the coin inside the bowl. You should still be able to reach the bowl. Stack a few books under the bowl if you can still see the coin. Then try this step again.

4. Write down what you see. Snap a photograph of the bowl. Or draw a picture.

5. Slowly pour water into the bowl. Watch to see what happens.

6. Write down what you see now. Take another photograph of the bowl. Or draw a new picture.

Review the Results

Read your experiment notes. Study any photos you took or pictures you drew. Did the water change what you saw? You could not see the coin before you added water. You could see the coin after water was added.

What Is Your Conclusion?

Water changes how light rays move. When the rays enter water, they slow down and bend. They hit the object in the water. Then the rays bounce out of the water. In the air again, the light rays speed up and bend back. When light bends, it is called **refraction**. The light rays bent over the edge of the bowl when water was in it. This is why you could see the coin.

It is easy to tell how an object changes light. Anything you can see through does not change light. Anything you cannot see through reflects light. Anything that makes other objects look bigger, smaller, or blurry bends light.

Refraction makes this straw look different underwater.

You need at least one eye to see.

14

CHAPTER FOUR

Yes, Eye Do!

Animals and people have at least two eyes. Some animals have many more eyes. But no animal has only one eye. Try this to see if two eyes are better than one.

Research the Facts

Here are a few. What other facts can you find?

- The eye moves in many directions. This is your **field of vision**.
- Your brain knows the size of an object. That is how the brain can tell how far away an object is.

Ask Questions

- Do we see better with two eyes than with one?
- What happens when we see with just one eye?

Make a Prediction

Here are two examples:

- People see better with two eyes than with one eye.
- People see the same with one or two eyes.

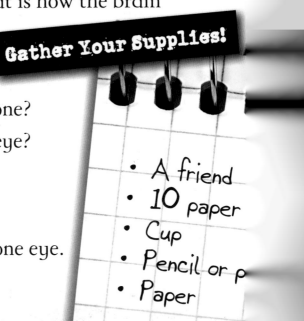

Gather Your Supplies!

- A friend
- 10 paper
- Cup
- Pencil or p
- Paper

Time to Experiment!

1. Ask your friend to stand behind a table. Your friend should place the cup on the table.
2. Take five steps back from the table. The cup and table should be between you and your friend.
3. Cover one of your eyes with your hand. Keep it covered.
4. Ask your friend to hold a paper clip 2 feet (0.6 m) above the table. Your friend should slowly move the paper clip around the table.
5. When you think the paper clip is above the cup, say, "Stop." Your friend should stop moving the paper clip and then drop it.

6. Repeat steps 4 and 5 with the rest of the paper clips. Try to get as many paper clips into the cup as you can. Write down what happens.

7. Repeat the experiment. This time do not cover either eye. Write down what happens.

Review the Results

Study your notes. Did you get more paper clips into the cup with one eye? Or was using two eyes better? It should have been easier to do with two eyes than with one.

What Is Your Conclusion?

Each eye works well on its own. But both eyes work together to help you see better. Each eye sees an object in a different way. So each eye sends a different picture to your brain. Your brain looks at both pictures. It can tell the difference. This helps you know how far an object is from you. With one eye covered, your brain has only one picture to work with. You cannot tell how far away an object is.

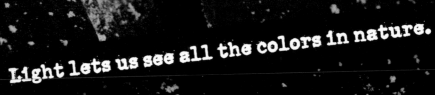

18

Light lets us see all the colors in nature.

CHAPTER FIVE

Lightly Colored

Light is all around us. It lets us see the bright purple of a flower or the rich green of grass. Try this to see if light is a color.

Research the Facts

Here are a few. What does your research show?

- Light passes through some objects. It bounces off other objects.
- Rainbows form in the sky. They have many colors. You can see a rainbow after it has rained.

Ask Questions

- Where do colors come from?
- What does light do to the colors we see?

Make a Prediction

Here are two examples:

- There is no color in sunlight.
- There are many colors in sunlight.

Time to Experiment!

- Adult help
- Shoebox with lid
- Utility knife
- Old CD
- Strong tape
- Scissors
- Clear tape
- Pencil or pen
- Paper

1. Ask an adult for help. Cut a hole on one of the small sides of the shoebox with a utility knife. The hole should be a rectangle. Make it about 1/8 inch (.3 cm) wide by 1.5 inches (4 cm) tall.

2. Cut a hole at the other end of the shoebox. The hole should be about the size of a quarter.

3. Look inside the box. Do you see any colors? Record what you see in your notes.

4. Cover the label side of the CD with strong tape. Press the tape onto the CD. Quickly pull the tape off. This should take off some of the coating on the disc.

5. Repeat step 4 until most of the label is gone.

6. Ask an adult for help. Cut off a piece of the CD. It should be a little bigger than a quarter.

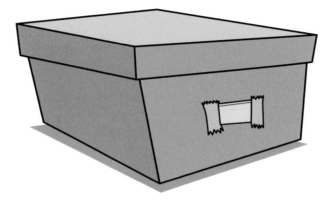

7. Tape the piece of CD over the hole made in step 2. Make sure the CD covers the hole. The bottom of the CD should face into the box.

8. Put the lid on the box. Point the open hole at light. This could be a window on a bright day. Do not point it at the sun!

9. Look through the piece of CD. Do you see colors? Write down what you see.

Review the Results

Look over your notes. Light went into the box. It reflected off the CD. You could see a rainbow of colors.

What Is Your Conclusion?

Light is made up of wavelengths. The wavelengths move at different speeds. This is called their **frequencies**. You see each frequency as a different color. The light reflects off the CD. The CD makes each frequency show on its own. The different frequencies shine onto the walls of the shoebox. They go in different directions. This lets you see the different colors in light.

What you built is called a **spectroscope**. Scientists use spectroscopes to look at the stars.

You can see colors as light reflects off a CD.

CHAPTER SIX

Beautiful in Black

Are there colors in black?

Black is a color. But is black just black? Learn about colors and how we see them.

Research the Facts

Here are a few. What else do you know?

- Light hits an object. But the object only reflects certain wavelengths. A blue object only reflects the part of light that is blue.

- We see the light that reflects off an object. That is how we see its color.

Ask Questions

- Is black made from other colors?
- What happens to black ink in water?

Make a Prediction

Here are two examples:

- Black is not made from any other colors.
- Black is a mix of different colors.

Gather Your Supplies!

- Coffee filter
- Black marker (water **soluble**)
- Pipe cleaner
- Scissors
- Cup of water
- Pencil or pen
- Paper
- Camera (optional)

Time to Experiment!

1. Draw a black dot in the middle of the coffee filter. Use the black marker.

2. Draw four to six larger dots in a circle around the middle dot. Use the black marker.

3. Cut a piece of pipe cleaner. Make it about 2 inches (5 cm) long. Poke the pipe cleaner through the middle dot on the coffee filter. Push the pipe cleaner about halfway through the hole.

4. Set the coffee filter and pipe cleaner on top of the cup of water. Make sure that the pipe cleaner is in the water. But keep the coffee filter dry.

5. Watch what happens. It may take a while. Write down what you see. Take pictures if you have a camera.

Review the Results

Read your notes. Look at your photographs. What happened as the black dots got wet? The ink spread out on the coffee filter. The black became different colors.

What Is Your Conclusion?

Were you right? Black is made from many different colors. The ink **dissolved** in the water. It spread across the coffee filter with the water. The ink showed the colors hidden inside black. This does not just work on black. Try it with other colored markers.

All of the colors we see are mixes of three colors. They are red, yellow, and blue.

You are a scientist now. What fun facts did you learn about light and vision? You learned that we see objects when light rays reflect off them. You saw that sometimes those rays bend. You can learn even more about light and vision. Study them. Experiment with them. Then share what you learn about light and vision.

Glossary

conclusion (kuhn-KLOO-shuhn): A conclusion is what you learn from doing an experiment. Her conclusion is that light can be seen in water.

dissolved (di-ZOLVD): Something that is dissolved seems to disappear when mixed with a liquid. The ink dissolved in the water.

experiment (ek-SPER-uh-ment): An experiment is a test or way to study something to learn facts. This experiment will show you how light rays bend.

field of vision (FEELD OF VIZH-uhn): Your field of vision is the total area you see with your eyes when you look at something. Your field of vision is less with only one eye.

frequencies (FREE-kwuhn-seez): Frequencies are the number of vibrations each second in light or sound waves. The frequencies of light have different colors.

prediction (pri-DIKT-shun): A prediction is what you think will happen in the future. His prediction that black is made from one color was wrong.

reflect (ri-FLEKT): To reflect is to bounce off an object. You see light reflect off objects.

refraction (ri-FRAKT-shun): Refraction is when light waves move through something and change direction. Refraction can show the colors in light.

soluble (SOL-yuh-buhl): Something that is soluble can dissolve in water. Some kinds of ink are soluble.

spectroscope (SPEK-truh-scope): A spectroscope is a tool that you can use to see the colors in light. Scientists can see stars with a spectroscope.

wavelengths (WAYV-lengthz): Wavelengths are the distances between one crest and the next in sound or light waves. Light waves have wavelengths.

Books

Bekkering, Annalise. *Sight: World of Wonder.* New York: Weigl Publishers, 2009.

Trumbauer, Lisa. *All About Light.* New York: Children's Press, 2004.

Weiss, Ellen. *The Sense of Sight.* New York: Children's Press, 2009.

Index

Web Sites

Visit our Web site for links about light and vision experiments:
childsworld.com/links

Note to Parents, Teachers, and Librarians: We routinely verify our Web links to make sure they are safe and active sites. So encourage your readers to check them out!

ABOUT THE AUTHOR:
Ryan Jacobson is the author of nearly 20 books, including picture books, chapter books, graphic novels, choose-your-path books, and ghost stories. He lives in Mora, Minnesota, with his wife Lora, sons Jonah and Lucas, and dog Boo.